Just Me

By Brenda "bjai" Clayburn
Illustrated by Sergio Drumond

Just Me
Text Copyright © 2020 by Brenda "bjai" Clayburn
Illustrations © 2020 by Sergio Drumond

All rights reserved. No part of this book may be reproduced or transmitted in any form or by any means, electronic or mechanical, including photocopying, recording, or by any information storage and retrieval system, without written permission from the publisher. The only exception is brief quotations for reviews.

For information address:
J2B Publishing LLC
4251 Columbia Park Road
Pomfret, MD 20675
www.J2BLLC.com
GladToDoIt@gmail.com

Printed and bound in the United States of America.
Designed by Sergio Drumond.

ISBN: 978-1-948747-78-3

This book is dedicated to all the children
who know they're special
and to all the children who don't.

"Being able to love ourselves will enable
us to love others like God loves us."
— Li Carol

Hello, my name is Kaleigha!

Momma says I'm really special
and I believe she's right,
she tells me this every time
she kisses me goodnight.
It's because I'm .... just me!

My elbows and knees
are "just right round"
and I love my skin,
it's pretty and it's brown –
it's perfect for ... just me!

I'm tall and skinny
and love my lips,
just the perfect size
for the perfect kiss!
And they were created for ... just me!

My big, fluffy hair
is so much fun –
it flounces and bounces
when I run.
And it's perfect for ... just me!

My hair when braided
lays perfectly straight,
its rows and patterns
make me feel great!
And God gave it to ... just me!

Friends say I talk too much –
that's absolutely true!
There's so much I want to say
and talking is what I do,
because I'm ... just me!

When Grandpa sings his funny songs
I dance and jump around.
I ask him why he laughs so loud,
he says because I'm such a clown!
Because I was being .... just me!

When Grandma shows me baby pictures
she hugs me really tight,
then she says she loves me best,
she tells me day and night!
Because I am .... just me!

I can pretend to be a princess,
and wear a glittery dress
but when I grow up, I'll still be special
because I'm very blessed.
And I'll always be .... just me!

Maybe one day, I'll save the world,
be a stupendous superstar!
Or a hula hooper on the moon
or an astronaut that travels far.
I think I'd rather be .... just me!

Some people say I'm a little loud
and I should quiet down,
but my inside part is very noisy,
I want you to hear my sound!
It's what makes me ... just me!

I may not be a princess yet
With a glittery dress to twirl,
or an astronaut or superstar
and I may not save the world
But, it's okay! I'm still ... just me!

My mom agrees I'm noisy,
my dad says I talk a bunch
but they tell me I am special,
and remind me I'm loved so much!
Because I'm .... Just me!

Bjai has a heart for encouraging children to be confident in God's love for them and purpose for their life. She is a children's pastor, the owner of *Milk and Honey Daycare*, and a teacher at the College of Southern Maryland.

When she started writing books, she knew she wanted to use them to teach and encourage younger generations.

Her first children's book, *Little Willie Wampel*, teaches children to acknowledge differences while enjoying the new people we meet.

Just Me encourages children to be comfortable with how God made them and to enjoy who they are.

Sergio Drumond is a painter and illustrator, with various degrees in Fine Arts and Advertising Art. His portfolio includes illustrating for books and magazines, graphic novels, newspapers and television. He lived in Europe where he worked on book illustrations and magazines as well as posters for theater companies. He spent most of his life in Asia, in such places as the Philippines, Japan, India and Thailand, where he worked illustrating books and graphic novels, and teaching art as support to non-profit institutions.

Made in the USA
Coppell, TX
17 February 2024